The Leaving Morning

story by **ANGELA JOHNSON**   *paintings by* **DAVID SOMAN**

Orchard Books   New York

J
J

Orchard Books, 95 Madison Avenue, New York, NY 10016

Manufactured in the United States of America. Printed by Barton Press, Inc.
Bound by Horowitz / Rae. Book design by Mina Greenstein

The text of this book is set in 18 point ITC Leawood Medium.
The illustrations are watercolor paintings, reproduced in full color.
10 9 8 7 6 5 4 3 2 1

Library of Congress Cataloging-in-Publication Data
Johnson, Angela.   The leaving morning / story by Angela Johnson ; paintings by
David Soman.   p.   cm.   "A Richard Jackson book"—P.
Summary: On the leaving morning, a child watches for the moving men, has a cup
of cocoa in the deli across the street, and leaves lip marks on the window of the
apartment before departing for the new home.
ISBN 0-531-05992-8.   ISBN 0-531-08592-9 (lib. bdg.)
[1. Moving, Household—Fiction.]   I. Soman, David, ill.   II. Title.   PZ7.J629Le
1992 [E]—dc20   91-21123   CIP   AC

To SANDY PERLMAN
and good times

—A.J.

To EUGENIE,
a restless family member

—D.S.

THE LEAVING happened on a soupy, misty morning,
when you could hear the street sweeper.
Sssshhhshsh....

We pressed our faces against the hall window and left cold lips on the pane.

It was the leaving morning.
Boxes of clothes,
toys,
dishes,
and pictures of us everywhere.

The leaving had been long because we'd packed
days before and said good-bye
to everybody we knew....

Our friends....

The grocer....

Everybody in our building....

And the cousins, especially the cousins.

We said good-bye to the cousins all day long.

Mama said the people in a truck would move us
and take care of everything we loved,
on the leaving morning.

We woke up early and had hot cocoa from the deli
across the street.
I made more lips on the deli window
and watched for the movers on the leaving morning.

We sat on the steps and
watched the movers.
They had blue moving clothes on
and made bumping noises on the stairs.
There were lots of whistles
and "Watch out, kids."

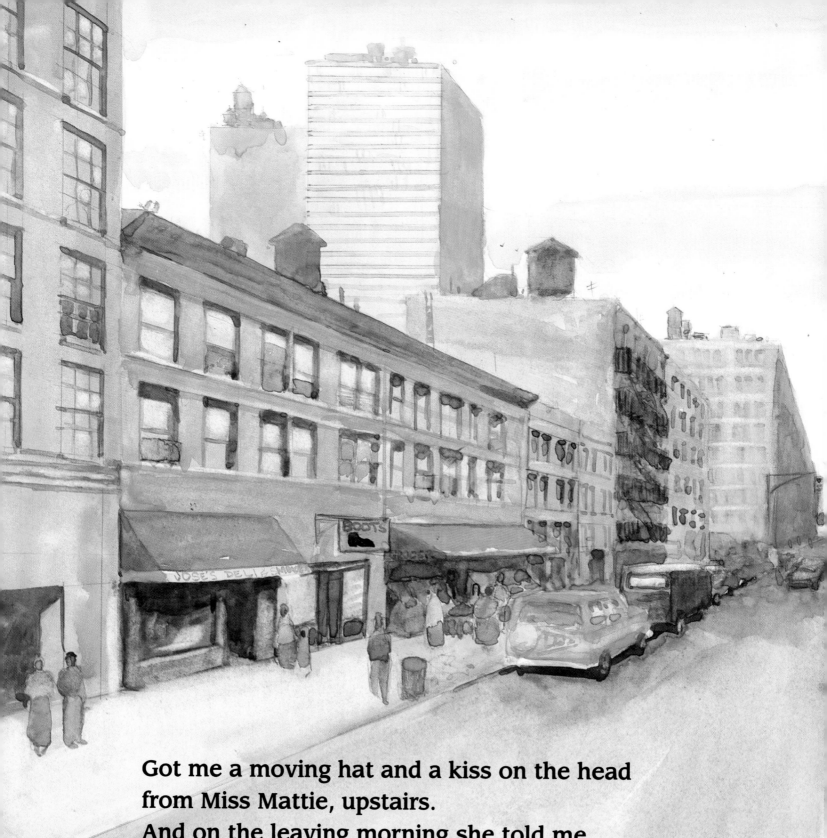

Got me a moving hat and a kiss on the head
from Miss Mattie, upstairs.
And on the leaving morning she told me
to watch myself in the new place when I crossed
the street, and think of her.

I sat between my mama and daddy,
holding their hands.
My daddy said in a little while we'd be someplace
we'd love.

So I left lips on the front window of our apartment,
and said good-bye to our old place,
on the leaving morning.